D1635619

The Sleepover Club

Have you been invited to all these sleepovers?

1. The Sleepover Club at Frankie's
2. The Sleepover Club at Lyndsey's
3. The Sleepover Club at Felicity's
4. The Sleepover Club at Rosie's
5. The Sleepover Club at Kenny's
6. Starring the Sleepover Club
7. The Sleepover Girls go Spice
8. The 24 Hour Sleepover Club
9. The Sleepover Club Sleeps Out
10. Happy Birthday, Sleepover Club
11. Sleepover Girls on Horseback
12. Sleepover in Spain
13. Sleepover on Friday 13th
14. Sleepover Girls at Camp
15. Sleepover Girls go Detective
16. Sleepover Girls go Designer
17. The Sleepover Club Surfs the Net
18. Sleepover Girls on Screen
19. Sleepover Girls and Friends
20. Sleepover Girls on the Catwalk
21. The Sleepover Club Goes for Goal!
22. Sleepover Girls go Babysitting
23. Sleepover Girls go Snowboarding
24. Happy New Year, Sleepover Club!
25. Sleepover Club 2000
26. We Love You Sleepover Club
27. Vive le Sleepover Club!
28. Sleepover Club Eggstravaganza
29. Emergency Sleepover
30. Sleepover Girls on the Range
31. The Sleepover Club Bridesmaids
32. Sleepover Girls See Stars
33. Sleepover Club Blitz
34. Sleepover Girls in the Ring
35. Sari Sleepover
36. Merry Christmas Sleepover Club

The Sleepover Club at Lyndsey's

TOO SCARED
TO SLEEP

by Rose Impey

Collins
An imprint of HarperCollinsPublishers

The Sleepover Club ® is a registered trademark
of HarperCollins*Publishers* Ltd

First published in Great Britain by Collins in 1997
Collins is an imprint of HarperCollins *Publishers* Ltd
77-85 Fulham Palace Road, Hammersmith,
London W6 8JB

The HarperCollins website address is
www.fireandwater.com

9 11 13 15 14 12 10 8

Text copyright © Rose Impey 1997

ISBN 0 00 675234 9

The author asserts the moral right to
be identified as the author of the work.

Printed and bound in Great Britain by
Omnia Books Limited, Glasgow

You are invited to Lyndsey Collins's
birthday sleepover and video party.

It is at Lyndsey's house:

The Orchards
Sash Lane
Little Wearing
Nr Cuddington
Leicester

It is on Friday 18 October.
Please come at 6 o'clock.

There will be lots of things happening.
After the food there will be a fashion show
and then video-watching. Then sleepover and
go home around 11 o'clock the next day!

There will be five people coming:
Frankie, Kenny, Fliss, Rosie and me.

from **Lyndz**

SLEEPOVER KIT LIST

1. Sleeping bag
2. Pillow
3. Pyjamas or a nightdress
4. Slippers
5. Toothbrush, toothpaste, soap etc
6. Towel
7. Teddy
8. A creepy story
9. Food for a midnight feast:
   chocolate, crisps, sweets, biscuits etc
10. A torch
11. Hairbrush
12. Hair things like a bobble or hairband,
    if you need them
13. Clean knickers and socks
14. A nice outfit (for the fashion show)
15. Sleepover diary

You must have your parents'
permission to see *Gremlins*!

CHAPTER ONE

Listen, don't tell anyone what I'm going to tell you. If it gets back to my mum and dad, I'm dead. So, when you've read this book... eat it.

OK, I was joking! But seriously, I mean *seriously*, I bet you never thought you'd hear me say this: *sometimes parents do know best!*

They did try to warn us. But you know grown-ups: they always try to talk you out of anything exciting you want to do. So, of course, we took no notice. And I suppose we were a bit OTT, because it was the first time we'd been allowed to sleep over since all the trouble with Brown Owl.

But *this* story is about Lyndsey's birthday party and what happened when we all slept over at her house and watched a scary video. We'd have been fine if Kenny hadn't started us off telling horror stories and then talking to ghosts. After that we were all too scared to sleep. So we were still awake in the middle of the night, when the bedroom door creaked open and *someone* came into the room...

But before I get started I suppose I'd better tell you who everyone is. I've got a photo of us somewhere. Ta-daaa! The Sleepover Club.

That's me in the middle: Francesca Thomas, but you can call me Frankie.

Next to me – on my right – is my best friend Laura McKenzie. She's the wild one; we call her Kenny.

That's Fliss on the end – Felicity Sidebotham, or, as the boys at school call her, Flossy *Slidebottom*.

Lyndsey Collins is on the other side of me. You remember her, she's the hiccup queen. We call her Lyndz.

And the last one's Rosie Cartwright. Rosie's just moved in round here. We don't really know her very well yet, but she seems OK, so far.

So that's all of us.

Mostly we sleep over at each other's houses at weekends or in the holidays. But best of all are special times like

Bonfire Night or Hallowe'en. Or birthdays!

I've got to wait ages for mine; it's not until April. I'm Aries. My horoscope book says I'm a born leader – bold, brave, decisive and quick-witted. Yeah, that's me!

I'm really into horoscopes. My dad says they're a load of rubbish but then he's Taurus – the Bull! He's dead stubborn.

Fliss has already had her birthday. She's Virgo, which means she's a bit of a fusspot. Fliss likes everything just so! Her birthday sleepover was another adventure, but we won't go into that now.

Kenny and Rosie have to wait even longer for their birthdays. Kenny's Gemini, a real split personality, and Rosie's a crab. That just describes her – prickly on the outside and soft inside. But Lyndz is Libra, dead soft-hearted. Lyndz is the one who always makes the peace and tries to look after everyone. It was because she felt sorry for Rosie that we let her join the Sleepover Club in the first place.

Even when it came to her own birthday party, Lyndz was so busy trying to keep everyone happy she couldn't decide what *she* wanted to do. I thought we'd never get it sorted out. You can probably guess who was playing up, as usual – Fusspot Fliss.

CHAPTER TWO

OK, let me tell you how it all started. One day after school we were at netball practice. Well, we weren't doing much practising. We were waiting for Miss Burnie to find the key to the PE store. She's always losing things. We all like her but, boy, is she dozy! We usually spend the first ten minutes of practice time looking for the key, or her whistle, or her plimmies. Or her! Quite often we find her having a cup of tea in the staff room – she's forgotten it's Tuesday and we're outside, standing round, shivering. So this day we were leaning against the PE store, waiting for her.

We're all in the netball team now. I play Goal Shooter and, even if I say so myself, I'm an ace shooter. Kenny's Goal Attack and together we're a pretty dynamic duo. Lyndz is Goal Defence and Fliss is Centre. But now Rosie's come and she plays Centre too. So that spells t-r-o-u-b-l-e.

At the moment she's in the second team but Miss Burnie's promised to try her out for the first team soon. Fliss isn't happy about it, I can tell you.

I said to Fliss, "Why don't you swap with Rosie and play Wing Attack?" But you know Fliss. She looked at me as if I'd suggested she cut her arm off.

"Why don't *you* swap with Rosie, if you think it's such a good idea?" she said.

"Because Rosie isn't a shooter," I said.

Rosie sort of looked down and said, "Don't worry. I don't care anyway." Which is a big fat porky-pie. You can see she wants to be in the first team like the rest of us, but she wouldn't admit it even if we put her in a bath of snails.

"Listen," I said, "if Rosie was in the first team, we could get rid of Alana Banana."

"Yeah. Four-one!" said Kenny, who can't stand her.

She's not really called that. Her name's Alana Palmer. She is too boring to live. She sometimes hangs around with the M&Ms. The M&Ms are two girls in our class: Emma Hughes and Emily Berryman. They are *so* stuck-up. They're teacher's pets and Brown Owl's pets and everybody-in-the-world's pets and we can't stand them, but fortunately the M&Ms can't play netball.

"I don't see why *I* should swap," said Fliss.

We were definitely heading for one of our arguments. So Lyndz, the peacemaker, changed the subject.

"I can't decide what to do for my birthday and it's only two weeks away."

"Surely we'll have a sleepover?" said Kenny.

"Yeah, but we've got to do something else as well," said Lyndz.

"Let's go skating," I said.

"Let's have a video," said Kenny.

"We could have *Babe*," said Fliss. "It's so sweet."

I said, "We've all seen that."

"Let's get a horror video," said Kenny. "One of the Freddy films."

"Yeah! They're great," said Rosie.

"How do you know?" I said.

"I've seen them."

"I bet you haven't," said Lyndz.

We knew Rosie was telling whoppers. It turned out she'd only seen the credits before her mum sent her to bed.

"Anyway," said Fliss, "you all know I

don't like horror films."

"Look, this is Lyndsey's birthday," I said. "It's up to her to choose what she wants."

"Well, if she does choose a horror film, I won't be able to come, and I don't think that's very fair, do you?"

Fliss is always talking about what's fair and making us vote on things. But sometimes it doesn't matter whether it's fair or not. It's like my gran says, you can't please everyone. I think when it's your birthday you should please yourself. That's what I'd have done.

But Lyndz is different. "I don't mind what we get."

"*Babe*," said Fliss again.

"We've *seen* it," I said, through gritted teeth.

Lyndz shrugged. "I don't mind."

Well, I minded and I was about to say so when Miss Burnie turned up with the key. So then netball practice started and there was no more time to talk.

But later I phoned Kenny to tell her what I thought about it. I always ring Kenny if I want a moan. Sometimes we talk for hours. But sometimes, if she's in one of those on-another-planet moods, I might as well save my breath to cool my porridge, as my gran says. This was one of *those* times.

I could tell she wasn't listening because I could hear the TV channels in the background. I could just see her sitting on the sofa with the mobile phone in one hand and the remote in the other, channel-hopping. She does it all the time. It drives her mum and dad barmy. And me. So I made her turn the sound down at least.

"*Listen*," I said. "Fliss is always going on about things not being fair. But this is Lyndz's birthday. If she wants to see a horror film and the rest of us want to see a horror film, we should see a horror film, shouldn't we? But we're not, are we? We're going to see *Babe*, whi we've all seen already. And why are we seeing it again? Because Fliss wants to see it again, that's why. Now you tell me, where's the fairness in that?"

"Search me. Gotta go, Frankie, *Rugrats* is on."

"Oh, thanks for nothing. I'll ring you again."

"OK. Bye."

See what I mean? Waste of time, or what? So then I rang Lyndsey.

"Hi, it's Frankie."

"Hi."

"I've been thinking about your birthday."

"Oh, yeah?"

"I was thinking, if you really want a horror film..."

"I don't mind."

"Don't keep saying that. It's your ▯hday, you should choose."

▯ have to ask my mum and dad."

▯ think about it, that's all."

I didn't really expect her to take any notice, so I was pretty surprised after tea when Lyndz rang me back, dead excited.

"Frankie, is that you? I've asked my mum and dad. Do you want the good news?"

"Yes. Go on."

"They didn't say no."

"That's supposed to be good news? But did they say yes?"

"No... but they didn't say no. Don't worry, I'll work on them."

CHAPTER THREE

And she must have done, because a few days later they said, "Maybe. We'll see. As long as it's suitable for children."

"Oh, great big hairy deal," said Kenny. "If they're anything like my mum and dad, they think *Tom and Jerry* ought to have a 15 certificate."

The trouble was we'd watched ᵥything PG that was worth watching

"I think they might let us see *Gremlins*," said Lyndz.

"Wicked!" said Rosie. "I saw that when Tiff and her boyfriend got it out."

Tiff is Rosie's older sister, she's fifteen. Perhaps Rosie had seen it, but we were getting used to her stories. We gave her our zip-fastener look. Up and down, dead fast.

"OK," she said, looking a bit sheepish, "I saw the first bit. They're dead-cute little furry things; really adorable. This man brings one home as a Christmas present for his son, but he forgets the rules and it gets wet and it makes lots more gremlins. Then he forgets the other rule and feeds them after midnight and that's when they turn nasty. *Then* I got sent to bed. Tiff said they were jumping out on people and getting them by the throat. One gets shut in the microwave and explodes all over the door."

"Oh, thanks, Rosie," I said. "Now

don't need to bother seeing the film."

"Sounds brilliant," said Kenny.

"Sounds *gruesome*," said Fliss.

"I don't want anything *too* scary," said Lyndz. "Just scary enough."

I agreed with Lyndz. I didn't want anything *too* scary. When I'm with my friends I love getting that shivery feeling, like when you go to Alton Towers and your stomach seems to have gone for a walk somewhere and there's this empty space where it used to be and you all scream and scream **really loud**. That is coo-el. It's the best.

But sometimes, when I'm on my own, if I see something horrible on TV or read something scary in a book, it sort of sticks in the back of my mind. When I go to bed, the minute I turn out the light, it p and then I can't stop thinking t. I lie there and I know it isn't it *feels* real as if it's in the room So I have to go downstairs and pretend I need a drink or I'm feeling a bit sick or something so my mum'll give me a cuddle.

I don't tell her the real reason I need a cuddle. No way. I know what she'd say: "I've *told* you not to watch programmes like that. You know they give you nightmares." *Or*, "Well, what do you expect, reading Bonechillers and Nightmares? At your age!"

But until you've seen something or read about it, how can you know if it's going to scare you? You can't, can you?

If I try to tell her I read scary stories because I like them, she looks at me as if I'm seriously weird. Just-scary-enough is brilliant. It's the best. But too scary is... *too scary*! You know what I mean.

The worst thing for me is *blood*. Kenny and me are total opposites. I'm really squeamish. So's my mum. It just makes us want to faint, or throw up. I don't mind reading about it, but I hate seeing it. It's gross.

But, listen, I don't want you telling the others about this. They think I'm the cool one. And most of the time I am. So keep it to yourself, all right?

Anyway, in the end Lyndz said she'd check it out with her brother Tom. He's really into horror. "I'll see what he thinks."

"Well, tell him we want something really gory with lots of blood in it," said Kenny.

Honestly, sometimes I think she must have been a vampire in another life.

Fliss was starting to look sick just talking about it. Fliss is worse than me. Much worse. She nearly passes out if she gets a splinter. And she's always having nightmares. She's the only person I know who screamed to come out of the cartoon of *Winnie-the-Pooh*. You know the bit where he gets stuck in Rabbit's hole and then comes out with a big POP! She *was* only three at the time, but she hasn't got much better.

But we were all starting to feel really bad about Fliss being left out and everything.

"Listen," I said, "just because you don't want to watch the film doesn't mean you can't come to the sleepover."

"No, of course not," said Lyndz.

"And what am I going to do while you're all watching it?" she snapped.

"We'll think of something," said Kenny.

But it wasn't Kenny's idea that she should sit in the corner with a woolly hat pulled over her eyes, which is what she did do. She came up with that idea all by herself. But then that's Fliss, nutty as a fruit cake, as my gran says.

CHAPTER FOUR

I'll tell you a bit about Lyndsey and her funny family next. When I say funny I mean funny-nice, not funny-horrid. They're really friendly and a great laugh, but they are a bit weird. And even more weird is Lyndsey's house.

Her dad's an art and design teacher and he's always redesigning their house, adding rooms or moving the stairs or the doors. One time when I went round I couldn't find the doorbell. The doorway was bricked up and the front door was round the side. Lyndz says sometimes even she can't find her way in.

At the moment her dad's building a new bedroom in the roof. Her baby brother needs a room of his own now, so he's going to have Lyndz's and she's having a new one, which will be great – more room for us when we sleep over. Her bedroom's so small the only way we can all get in is to take the bed out and lay our sleeping bags side by side on the floor as if we're playing Sardines. It's good fun, though.

Lyndz's mum used to teach art as well but now she teaches women how to have babies. She knows a lot about it; she's had five herself. Apart from Lyndz, they're all boys. That's why she likes it when *we* sleep over. She says it makes a nice change having a house full of girls after all those smelly boys!

Stuart's the oldest, he's sixteen. He's

mad about farming and he wants to go to agricultural college. But he's re-sitting his exams at the moment.

Tom's fourteen and he's *gorgeous*. Well, we used to think he was, before the sleepover! Lyndz says there're always girls from his class hanging around outside or ringing him up. He's into computer graphics and horror.

Lyndsey's in the middle. A rose between four thorns, her dad says.

Ben's four and a real little toughy. He's always jumping on you from behind and wanting to wrestle.

And then there's the baby, Sammy, but they call him Spike, because he's got this little tuft of hair which sticks up. He's six months old and just starting to crawl. You have to watch him like a hawk. He's always getting into places he shouldn't, which isn't difficult in that house.

Because she's got such a big family and all that building going on, Lyndz's mum's too busy to fuss about things like what time you go to bed or whether you've had a proper wash or how many biscuits you're allowed, you know the kind of thing. So sleepovers at Lyndz's are always great fun.

One of the best things about staying at Lyndz's is the fave set of dressing-up clothes she's got. Her mum had some of them when *she* was little. There are long dresses and cloaks and hats and belts and shoes and bags. Everything. We have mega dressing-up sessions and fashion shows. We use the back stairs to the attic as a catwalk, with Oasis playing really loud, pretending we're super-models.

That's another good thing about Lyndz's house – we can make a noise. Her mum's used to it, they're a pretty noisy family and Lyndz is the noisiest. We call her Slush Bucket, she's so noisy when she drinks. She giggles really loud too and when she gets hiccups you can nearly hear her in the next street.

But on the night of her birthday sleepover we'd been warned – on pain of death – not to wake her mum and dad up. With the baby they don't get much sleep. So even when we started to get really scared, we didn't dare go and get them. We just hid at the bottom of our sleeping bags. Well, so would you have done. Believe me, it was seriously scary.

Hang on. Before I tell you any more we'd better check no one's listening. My house isn't like Lyndz's. You can't be too careful round here. Walls have ears and so does my mum! Let's go down into the garden. If we see her, act natural. Be cool. My mum's a real Inspector Clouseau.

OK, you sit on the swing and I'll tell you the rest.

By the time her birthday came, Lyndz had managed to get round her mum and dad. They said yes, we could watch

Gremlins as long as...
1. It wasn't too scary. (Tom promised them it wasn't.)
2. It wasn't sexy. (P-lease!) (Tom told them it definitely wasn't.)
3. We all had our parents' permission. (Fliss wasn't going to be watching it, but she still needed permission, anyway.)
4. Lyndz paid for it out of her birthday money. (She said OK.)

And, most important of all:
5. If we scared ourselves out of our brains watching it, we'd better not keep them awake all night, or we wouldn't be worth a prayer!

"It's a deal," said Lyndz.

Then the rest of us had to persuade our parents. I thought it would be a piece of cake persuading mine. How wrong can you be?

"*Gremlins*?" said my mum. "I'm not sure about that. It's a 15, isn't it?"

"Fifteen! She'll be wanting to go to

raves next," said my dad.

"... and drinking..." said Mum.

"... and smoking."

My mum and dad think they're funny, but they're not. And they go on... and on...

"She'll be sniffing Pritt sticks..."

"... staying out all night..."

Honestly, what are they like? "It's only a video," I said. "Please!" I put on my most adorable Andrex-puppy face. I begged and pleaded and whined...

"All right! All right!" said Mum in the end. "Just this once."

Yeah! Four-one! I jumped up and smothered her with kisses.

"But I don't want you coming home feeling ill because you were too scared to sleep."

"Don't worry," I said. "You know me."

"Exactly," said Dad, "that's the trouble."

"Remember, you've been warned," said Mum.

I said, "Yeah, yeah. Hang loose,

Mother Goose," which always winds her up.

So I left, sharpish. 5-4-3-2-1 and I was gone, before they changed their minds.

Lyndz's birthday was on a Friday, so that day at school we were all OTT. Mrs Weaver threatened to split us up a couple of times if we couldn't settle down and get on with some work.

Kenny had got the OK from her parents. Fliss's mum had made her promise *on her life* that she wouldn't so much as peep at the screen, which is stupid because you couldn't have persuaded Fliss to watch it if you'd promised her a year's supply of Mint Magnums. Rosie's mum's pretty laid back so she hadn't taken too much persuading. We were so excited we were jumping up and down.

"I can't wait for tonight," I said.

"It's gonna be so cool," said Rosie.

"It's gonna be so scary," said Lyndz, grinning.

"I hope there's plenty of blood," said Kenny. "I do lurv a bit of blood!"

"I just hope," said Fliss, "that when you all scare yourselves out of your pants you'll remember that I was against this from the start."

Yawn, yawn. She can be so bor-ing.

"Don't worry, I don't scare easy," said Kenny.

"Oh, don't you *now*!" I shouted, suddenly frightening them all out of their wits. They just about jumped out of their seats. Mrs Weaver gave us a warning look.

"Don't do that," said Rosie. "I nearly wet myself."

"It isn't funny," said Fliss, white in the face.

"No, Francesca, it's very infantile," said Kenny, putting on Mrs Weaver's voice. "You wouldn't like it if someone scared you half to death, now would you?"

Well, no, I s'pose I wouldn't. Actually,

that night something did scare me half
to death and I didn't like it one little bit.

CHAPTER FIVE

Lyndz told us to come for six o'clock and when we got there her mum had made a brilliant spread: hot dogs (vegetarian for me and Lyndz), jacket potatoes, crisps, curry salad (not so good), egg and banana sandwiches (no, not together), milkshakes, toasted marshmallows, fairy cakes, oh and lots of cucumber.

Cucumber is one of our fave foods:

cucumber sandwiches, cubes of cucumber and cheese on sticks, cucumber salad and grated cucumber with yoghurt, with lots of salt on it. We don't mind how we eat it, as long as there's lots of cucumber.

After we'd eaten we got dressed up. I bagged a long silky dress with big sleeves like a pair of wings and silver shoes with heels. I would die for those shoes. Lyndz won't give them to me; I already asked her. So I always grab them first.

Kenny's in love with this purple velvet jacket and flared pants. She looked pretty weird because she was wearing them over her Leicester City Football Club T-shirt, which she just about lives in.

Rosie dressed up as a Strawberry Flower Fairy, Fliss was a mermaid and Lyndz wore her grandma's wedding dress, which Fliss wanted, but then she remembered that it *was* Lyndz's birthday.

Then we went to watch the film.

As a special treat, Lyndz had persuaded Stuart to let us use his room. He's got his own TV and video, so we could watch the film in there, rather than in the living room, which is packed out with things like new floorboards and radiators for Lyndz's bedroom. And, even better, he said we could *sleep* in his room.

Stuart has this humungous bed. Well, it isn't a proper bed with legs or anything, just this huge mattress on the floor. I wish my mum and dad would let me sleep on the floor. It's really cool. All of us fitted on it, and it was bouncy like a trampoline.

Stuart had gone to a party at the Rugby Club and wouldn't be in till really late, so he said he'd sleep in Lyndz's bed, unless he stayed with one of his friends.

When Tom came in to set the video up for us, we were having a bouncing competition. I was winning, of course, because I'm so much bigger to start with. Once or twice I bounced into the lampshade.

"Right, are you lot ready?" said Tom.

We all did a few more bounces and then landed, sitting down in a row, facing the TV.

"Yeah! Good one!" shouted Kenny.

"Great timing," said Fliss.

"Synchronised bouncing!" I said. "That would make a brilliant new round for our International Gladiators contest."

"Stu must be mad," said Tom, shaking his head. "There's no way I'd let five weird women in my room. No way!"

"We're not women," Fliss giggled. "We're girls."

"And we're not weird," said Lyndz.

"That, little sister, is a matter of opinion. Are you sure you ought to watch this video? Isn't it a bit frightening for *little girls*?"

He grinned at us, but we all gave him

the evil eye and the cross of the vampire.

"Go away," said Lyndz.

"OK, OK, I'm going," he said, grinning. "But I may be back."

"Sssss," we hissed.

We all got comfy on Stuart's bed with our pillows behind us and a huge packet of popcorn between us. Fliss sat on her own, on a beanbag in the corner, with her back to the TV.

"Shall I turn it on?" said Lyndsey, with the remote ready in her hand.

"Not yet," said Fliss, taking out a green knitted hat and pulling it down over her face.

"You won't be able to breathe if you do that," said Lyndz.

"At least leave your mouth clear," said Rosie. "Then you can fit the popcorn in."

"She looks like a mugger," I whispered to Kenny.

"I heard that," said Fliss.

"Now are we ready?" said Lyndz.

"I'm not," said Rosie. "I need the loo."

I was glad Rosie had thought of it, because I knew I wouldn't dare go once the film had started. All the others must have thought the same, because then they all decided to go. But, at last, we really were ready.

We sat down on the bed close together, clutching hold of each other, grinning and squealing our heads off. And that was before Lyndz even switched it on!

Her dad put his head round the door, looking dead worried. "Are you lot all right?"

"It's OK, it hasn't started yet," said Lyndz.

"Well, just remember, we don't want you so overexcited you can't sleep. Is that understood?"

Yes, yes, we all nodded. We grinned at him. Lyndz said she'd had the same warning five times already that day.

Suddenly he spotted Fliss, sitting in the corner with a hood over her face.

"Felicity, are you sure you want to sit there like that all night? Why don't you come downstairs and watch something on TV?"

"No, it's all right, Dad," said Lyndz. "Fliss wants to stay with us."

"We're going to tell her what's happening," said Kenny.

"She just doesn't want to see it, that's all," I said.

Lyndz's dad shook his head. "And I thought boys were strange."

It was already quite dark. We couldn't decide whether to put the lights on or leave them off. It would be more spooky with them off, but we didn't want it *too spooky*. So we decided to keep Stuart's bedside light on, just in case.

You know! In case *anything* happened.

To tell you the truth, I was starting to feel a bit jumpy by now. Usually I don't mind the dark. I don't sleep with a light on, like some people. But it's more scary when you're in someone else's house. It wouldn't have felt quite so scary in Lyndz's room with all her horse pictures around us. But we'd never been in Stuart's room before.

I didn't say anything, though. I just tried to be Ms Cool. Dead laid back. Nothing worried me. Until the face at the window!

CHAPTER SIX

I'm telling you, we nearly jumped out of our skin. It was seriously scary. We just looked over and there was this face pressed up against the glass. It looked gruesome.

"Oh, my God!" said Rosie. "What's that?"

Fliss whipped off her hood and started to scream. "Help! Help! Mummy! Mummy!"

"Shhh," said Lyndsey. "It's only my stupid brother. You're going to get it when Dad finds out you've been messing about with his ladders," she shouted at him through the glass. That's what Lyndz's brothers are like: always playing tricks on her.

"He nearly frit me to death," said Fliss.

Lyndsey pulled the curtains closed. Tom started tapping and making stupid howling noises. "Just ignore him," she said.

"I think we should open the window and push him off," said Kenny.

"I think we should empty a bucket of water over his head," I said.

"I think you should go and tell your dad," said Fliss.

"You know I can't do that," Lyndz reminded her. "I promised them: no trouble, or else."

So we did ignore him and finally he went away.

"Come on," said Kenny. "Are we ever

going to watch this film?"

We were all a bit shivery and we hadn't even seen a gremlin yet. At first, Rosie was right, they just seemed cute. It's going to be really tame, I thought. But was I wrong!

Some films are like that. They sort of trick you into thinking, This is OK, I can handle this. But then it changes and you feel as if you're on a roller coaster that's going too fast and you wish you could get off. One minute the gremlins were all cuddly and sweet, sort of burbling and singing, the next they were hissing and spitting and talking like Daleks and bursting out of wardrobes with lasers, attacking people.

A couple of times I almost jumped out of my skin. I tried to tell myself, This is only a film, it isn't really happening. Somebody made them up. They don't exist. There's no such thing as a gremlin. But then I began to think, What if there is? Right here, in this town, in Lyndz's street, in Stuart's bedroom? Ahhh! I buried my head in my knees.

I was glad Rosie had warned us about the bit with the microwave. When it came on, I didn't watch it. Kenny did, of course. She kept up a running commentary for Fliss.

"Now she's turned it on and it's going round and round in it. Now it's exploded. It's gone splat! all over the door. There's blood everywhere."

"Don't tell me that!" squealed Fliss. "It's gross! I don't want to hear any more."

So Kenny stopped telling her, but then, when she could still hear the rest of us groaning, she said, "What's happening now? What's going on? Somebody tell me what's happening." You can't win with Fliss.

There were lots of bits I had to watch with my hands in front of my face. Rosie kept burrowing into me and trying to hide between me and the wall. Lyndz hid her face in Stuart's pillow. Only Kenny watched all of it, but then you know what she's like.

When it got really hairy we had to turn the big light back on. We all kept our feet tucked right under us, even though there was no room for anything to be hiding under Stuart's bed, unless it was dead thin, like the Flat Man.

Some bits were pretty funny, actually, in a stupid way. But other bits were terrifying.

Every time we thought they'd killed the last one off, more of them would leap out of the dark. And that started us off screaming and grabbing hold of each other again.

The screaming was the best bit. I loved it. But I didn't like the gruesome bits. The people who think up horror films must have really weird minds. They were probably like Kenny when they were kids. Seriously weird.

CHAPTER SEVEN

Uh-oh, look out! There's Nathan from next door, looking over the fence. He seems to think just because I go there after school to be *minded* by his mum, he can barge in even when I've got friends round. Ignore him. He's stupid.

"Get a life, Nathan. Go away! This is girls' talk."

Come on, we'll go over the other side of the garden. This bit's not for *his* ears.

After the film had finished, we were really hot and sweating with all that squealing.

Lyndz's mum looked in to check on us. "Well, did you enjoy that?"

"It was wicked," said Kenny.

"Coo-el," I said.

"I just hope it's not going to give you nightmares."

"No, we're fine, Mum," said Lyndsey. "I promise."

"Well, I hope so. Now, can you hurry up in the bathroom? Because I'd like a bath before I go to bed and I'd like it before midnight."

But when she'd gone, still nobody moved. I guess no one wanted to go down that long corridor from Stuart's room and right round the corner to the bathroom on their own. What if there were gremlins hiding behind the curtains, waiting at the top of the stairs, lurking in the bathroom? So we all started to get ready for bed instead.

The most important part of your sleepover kit is your sleeping bag and your pillow. Mine's a special one with Winnie-the-Pooh and Piglet walking in the snow on the pillowcase. It's not my regular pillow, it's an old one, so I'm allowed to use it for pillow fights. Kenny used to have an inflatable one. We used to blow it up really hard and sit on it, so the air rushed out and made rude noises, like a whoopee cushion. But once she blew it up so hard it burst. Now she has an ordinary one like the rest of us.

Stuart's bed was so big we could all fit on it but there was only room for four of us in a row, so someone had to sleep across the bottom with everyone's feet resting on them. We had a pillow fight to see who.

We swung them round and whacked each other with them and tried to knock each other off the bed. The last person left on the bed was the winner. We were right in the middle of it – Fliss and Rosie had been knocked out – when Lyndz's mum popped her head in and out.

"This is absolutely your *last* call for the bathroom," she said.

"OK, Mum," said Lyndsey.

We all flopped down on the mattress, exhausted.

"I'm too tired to move," said Kenny. "I think I'll stay mucky."

None of us likes washing much. It seems a waste of time being in the bathroom when you could be having a laugh with your friends.

"Oh, dear," I said, sniffing the air. "What is that odour?" I sniffed a path all the way to Kenny, like a bloodhound. "Ugh. Disgusting!"

"*You're* disgusting," said Fliss. She thinks it's so rude, talking about people smelling; the rest of us think it's a real laugh.

I pretended the smell had made me

faint and I rolled over on top of Kenny.

"Watch my bladder," she squealed. "I really need to go."

"Bladder!" said Lyndsey and started to shriek. "Bladder!"

Kenny just rolled her eyes and gave us a look. She's going to be a doctor, like her dad, when she grows up. She's always using words like "bladder".

"Well, go, if you want to go," said Fliss. But Kenny still didn't move.

None of us really wanted to go to bed. We wanted to keep the lights on and play all night. But it was late, nearly eleven o'clock. We started to get undressed.

When we get undressed at a sleepover, we always do it inside our sleeping bags. We wriggle down inside with our jimjams, then throw out our clothes, like we're doing the fastest striptease in the world, only no one can see us because we're inside our sleeping bags. Kenny's usually the fastest; I'm usually the last because I'm so big and, like my grandma says, all arms and legs and feet.

But the moment Lyndz crawled down into hers, she started screaming and scrambled out as if there was an alligator at the bottom. "Ugh, ugh! What's that?" she squealed.

Out came Buster, their little Jack Russell terrier. He's always curling up in funny places and going to sleep. He looked pretty annoyed to be woken up.

The poor dog ran to the door and whined to be let out.

"It was horrible!" said Lyndz. "I could feel something soft and warm and then he started licking my feet and it felt wet and yukky."

"It must have been far worse for him," I said, "having your big smelly feet land on his head."

Kenny found something at the bottom of hers too, but it was only her torch.

"Brillo! I thought I'd lost that. I've

been looking for it all week," she said.

She turned it on and held it under her chin. She pulled a terrible face and then said, in a creepy voice, "I know, let's read a scary story."

We always bring a scary book with us to sleepovers, but we'd read most of them before, and after that film they seemed pretty tame. So we decided to tell our own stories. Looking back on it now, we should have listened to Fliss.

"I don't want to do this," she said. "I might be sick."

"You won't be sick," said Rosie.

"Well, I'll have nightmares," she said. But Kenny said she couldn't have nightmares if she didn't go to sleep, and if she wanted we'd all stay awake with her.

After all, the whole point of sleepovers is *not* to go to sleep, isn't it?

"I still don't want to," said Fliss.

"Oh come on," said Kenny.

"Don't worry, we'll all be together,"

said Lyndz. "It'll be a laugh."

"You'll be all right," I said. "You can come in the middle, if you like."

So she dragged her sleeping bag between us and we got in really close around her.

"Someone put the light out," said Kenny.

"Do we have to have the light out?" Fliss started to whinge.

"Yes," said Kenny. "It won't be as good if we don't. We've got our torches."

So we all turned on our torches. I put out the light and then dived back into my place.

Lyndz said, "Frankie, you start."

"OK," I said. "Snuggle up close."

I could feel the others round me, shivering with excitement. It was wonderful. It felt scary, but in a good way – to begin with. But somehow things got a bit out of hand – well, more than a bit, actually.

CHAPTER EIGHT

Even if I say so myself, I tell the best stories. My gran says it's because I'm a bit of an actress. And I suppose I am. I'd love to be in films or on TV. I try to do it like our teacher, Mrs Weaver. She tells us brill stories, with all the voices and lots of expression. Not like Mr Short, our last teacher. He used to talk down his nose. He was bor-ing. We used to fall asleep when he read us anything.

But I do all the voices. I'm especially good at creepy voices. I know when to whisper and then, when everyone's leaning forward so they can hear, I suddenly shout and make them jump out of their skins, just when they're not expecting it.

I looked over my shoulder, as if *something* was already in the room with us, lurking in the shadows. I lowered my voice and whispered, "Prepare to meet ... the Blur!"

"Uh-oh," said Lyndsey, grinning. "Not the Blur!"

"Oh, no," said Fliss. "I don't like this."

"Shhhh," said the others.

The Blur is this character I invented. "It doesn't have a face," I told them, "it's just this shape that can pass through walls. It can slide through anything, even bullet-proof glass.

"Sometimes, when you think you've seen something out of the corner of your eye and then you look again real quick, and it's gone, that was the Blur."

"That's how fast it moves, like a flash. It just glides through anything and then hides, like a shape-shifter, pretending to be something ordinary and harmless. It might be hiding behind the curtains, or in the corner of the stairs, or behind the toilet door, or under your bed, or even in the bottom of your sleeping bag. It might be waiting for you right now," I said, dropping my voice even lower. "So be careful, or it might jump out and *get you*!"

"Don't *do* that!" said Fliss. "You'll make me sick."

"Yeah," said Lyndz. "You nearly scared me to death."

Rosie was clutching her throat. "Honestly, Frankie, you could have warned us."

"That was wicked," said Kenny. "My turn next. Erm, let me think…"

She shone her torch under her chin so that her whole face glowed, and when she grinned her eyes disappeared into two little slits. You could still tell it was Kenny, but she looked too ugly to live. It was gruesome. I could hardly bear to look at her.

"I know," she said. "I'll tell you about the Ghost Train."

I've heard this story before. Kenny's sister told it to her. She'd heard it at school. There's a little low bridge that goes over the railway line on Arthur Street. Well, years and years ago there was a big crash there and a train ploughed into the side of the bridge and every single person on the train was killed. Sometimes you're supposed to be able to hear the train whistle in the distance. And some people say that if you stay there until it comes under the bridge, you'll see it go by, full of ghosts.

Then you have to look away, really quickly because if they look you in the eye they'll pull you on board and then you'll turn into a ghost and be stuck on the train for ever.

Kenny started making ghost noises, but it sounded more like a steam train. We all started to giggle, but we soon stopped, because there was a knock on the wall.

"What was that?" said Fliss. "Oooh! I don't like it."

"It's OK," said Lyndz, putting her arm round Fliss's shoulders.

I said, "It's probably the Blur, knocking to come in." I grinned at Kenny. I guessed it was her knocking. We often play that game. But this time she looked back and shook her head as if it wasn't. Then there was another knock.

Rosie said, "Perhaps it's the Grey Lady, trying to make contact with us."

Do you ever play that game: White Lady, Grey Lady? Sometimes we throw a stone in the air and ask her questions. Or sometimes we knock on the floor and talk to her.

"Ask her something," said Lyndz.

I looked at Kenny. She still wasn't grinning, but she nodded.

"Is there anybody there?" I said in my spooky talking-to-ghosts voice. "Knock once for yes, twice for no."

"That's stupid," said Fliss. "How can she knock twice if she isn't there?"

"Shhh," said the others.

There was one knock.

"Ask her something else," said Rosie. "Ask if she's a friend."

"If you're a friend, knock once," I said. "If you're an enemy, knock twice."

There was one loud knock. We were all glad about that.

"Have you got a message for us?" I asked. "Knock once for yes."

There was another knock.

"Who's it for?" said Rosie.

I said, "If it's for me, Francesca Theresa Thomas, knock once. If it's for Rosie Cartwright, knock twice. If it's for Lyndsey Collins, knock three times. If it's for Kenny, I mean Laura McKenzie, knock four times. And if it's for Felicity Sidebotham, knock five times."

There was a long row of knocks.

"Five," gasped Lyndz. "It's for Fliss."

"I don't want it," said Fliss, wriggling down into her sleeping bag. "Tell her to go away. I don't want any messages." She was getting really worked up.

"Ask if she's got a message for someone else," said Rosie.

But I felt a bit like Fliss. I didn't really want to know. It's OK when you play games like this at school, in the daytime, but not in the dark. And I still couldn't work out who was doing the knocking, so I was starting to get a bit nervous. Rosie nudged me.

"Is there a message for anyone else?" I said.

There was no knock this time. We sat waiting in the torchlight for what seemed like ages. I could feel Lyndz holding on to me on one side and I could feel Fliss's nails digging into my other arm. We were all holding our breath, wondering what was going to happen. Kenny was grinning, but then she often does that when she's really nervous. It gets her into loads of bother at school. I started to shiver.

Suddenly the bedroom door flew open and in walked this tall lady.

CHAPTER NINE

She wasn't in grey, she was all in white, from the top of her head to her feet. Thank goodness, it was Lyndsey's mum in a long, white dressing gown with a towel round her hair. We nearly died of fright.

"Whatever's going on?" she said. "Who keeps knocking? You'll wake the baby up."

"It wasn't me, honest, Mum," said

Lyndsey. She looked at the rest of us, but no one spoke. We just shrugged and looked at each other.

I knew it wasn't me; I knew it wasn't Fliss. It had to be one of the other three leaning against the wall. But none of them owned up.

Lyndz's mum looked really fed up with us. "Fancy sitting here in the dark, after a film like that. I knew this would happen. You'll never get to sleep tonight, I can tell."

"We will, honest," said Lyndsey. "We're going to sleep now, Mum."

"I want no more knocking. Now, put those torches away and settle down, do you hear?"

"Yes, Mum."

"Good night."

We all muttered, "Good night."

She closed the door and we heard her go back to bed. We snuggled down into our sleeping bags and lay in the dark without a sound.

"I think we'd better go to sleep," Lyndz whispered.

"OK," Kenny whispered back.

"Good night," whispered Fliss.

We heard the church clock strike midnight. There wasn't a sound from the others. I really tried to go to sleep, but I just couldn't settle. *We still hadn't been to the bathroom.*

I couldn't wait any longer and I was about to say so when Fliss's voice came through the dark. "I'm dying for a wee and I'm too scared to go on my own."

"So am I."

"And me."

"I'm bursting," said Kenny. "It's giving me a pain."

"Let's all go together," I said.

We started to get out of our sleeping bags.

"What if there's anything out there?" said Fliss.

"What, like the Blur, you mean?" said Lyndz.

"Or gremlins," whispered Fliss.

"Gremlins aren't real," I said.

"But what if they are?"

"*They aren't!*" I insisted. "Now come on, let's stick together. Let's hold hands."

As we crept out of the bedroom, I was last and I grabbed hold of Stuart's tennis racquet, propped against the wall, just in case.

Yes, I know I told Fliss gremlins aren't real, but you can't be too careful.

We made our way along the landing to the bathroom in the little bit of light that shone through the landing window. We couldn't risk waking anyone by putting a light on. We'd have been in doom for ever.

Of course when we got there we had this big argument, in whispers, about who was going in first. Lyndz told us to be quiet or her mum would hear us, and anyway she was going in first, because *it was her birthday*!

I said, "It isn't, *actually*, it's gone midnight." But she'd already slipped in and closed the door.

By the time we'd hung around on the landing until *everyone* had been, we'd all got really cold in our jimjams and bare feet. So when we got back to the bedroom, we couldn't stop shaking. Fliss said she was feeling a bit sick and by now so was I.

It could have been all the popcorn we'd eaten. It could have been watching *Gremlins*. It could have been nearly jumping out of our skins when Lyndz's mum came in. Whatever it was, we were all starting to feel funny.

"Perhaps we'd better go to sleep," said Lyndz. "Fliss looks terrible."

She did. She was a funny green colour and her eyes had sunk into her head.

"OK," I said.

"I'm dead beat anyway," said Kenny.

"Yes, let's all go to sleep," said Rosie. But it wasn't that easy.

When it's a sleepover, we all have different ways of getting to sleep and we never agree on it. But the one thing we *always* do before we settle down is to sing our song. We have this sort of club song and we sit up in our sleeping bags and do it with the hand movements. I bet you know it.

"Down by the river there's a hanky-pankyyy,
With a bull-frog sitting near the hanky-pankyyy.
With an ooh-ah, ooh-ah, hey, Mrs Zippy, with a 1-2-3 OUT!"

And the first one to lie down flat on the word OUT! turns off her torch. Then we keep on going round until everyone's out. No one likes being last because then you're left sitting there almost in the dark and it's a bit creepy. That night it felt mega-creepy.

Fliss was the last one and then she

wouldn't turn her torch off because she said she was too scared to go to sleep unless the light was on. The trouble is, I can't get to sleep unless the light's out. So I made Fliss turn it off.

Kenny likes to hum to herself and make sort of snuffling noises. It drives her sister, Molly the Monster, mad. *And* she talks in her sleep. She says some potty things.

Rosie's just like our dog. When Pepsi wants to lie down, she has this funny routine where she goes round and round in circles scruffing up her bed until it's just how she likes it and then she flops down, curled up in a ball. Rosie does that. She tries out every position she can think of before she settles. She starts off on her back, then she turns on one side, then the other, then she rolls over on her stomach. We thought she was never going to settle down. We all yelled, "Rosie! Cut it out."

It was like trying to sleep on a bouncy castle.

The next thing, Fliss started to sniff. Then Kenny started up and then they all seemed to be playing pass the sniff.

"Pack it in," I said.

There was another sniff.

"Fliss!"

"It wasn't me," she said. "It must have been Kenny."

"It was not. It was Rosie."

There was one humongus sniff. "Sorry, sorry," said Fliss. "That *was* me. But I won't do it again. I've finished, honest."

Finally everyone was quiet. I was just dropping off when I heard Kenny say, "By the way, who was it, knocking on the wall?"

Suddenly I was wide awake. "I thought it was you," I said.

"It must have been Rosie."

Rosie said, "I thought it was Frankie."

"I'll bet it was Lyndz," said Kenny.

"Not guilty. Must have been Fliss."

"*It wasn't me!*" Fliss almost shrieked.

We all sat up in bed and turned our torches back on.

"So who was it? Come on, own up."

"*You* own up," said Fliss. "You're the one who does that kind of thing."

"Look, I'm telling the truth." And I licked my finger and made a cross on my chest. "Cross my heart and hope to die," I said.

So then everyone else licked their fingers, crossed their hearts and made the Brownie sign as well. Well, someone must be telling porky pies and I was going to find out who. I stared them in the eye, one by one. But this time no one blinked.

CHAPTER TEN

I don't know about you, but I hate mysteries. At least, I hate ones I can't solve. And then what I hate is that I can't stop thinking about them. You know what it's like when someone asks you if you can remember the words to a song or the name of a book or a character in it, and you can't. After a while they say, oh, never mind, and they just forget about it, but then *you* can't. And it drives you mad until you can remember. That happens to me all the time. My dad says it's because I'm stubborn and I won't let go of things.

Well, now I couldn't let go of this. I went through the possibilities. I *knew* it wasn't me knocking. I was *sure* it wasn't Fliss. It *wasn't* Lyndz, she would have owned up. So that left Rosie and Kenny. It could have been Kenny. I know she sometimes tells porkies, for a laugh, but she *usually* owns up in the end. So it must have been Rosie. I looked straight into her eyes, as if I could see inside her head and read her mind like a book. I was staring so hard my eyes began to water.

"Stop it," said Fliss. "You're frightening me."

"Yeah, pack it in," said Lyndz.

"I'm going to get to the bottom of this," I said, "because if it wasn't any of us knocking, you know what that means. It means that this house… is *haunted*."

But before any of them could speak, we heard noises: stairs creaking, footsteps coming along the landing, then stopping outside the bedroom door...

"Quick," whispered Lyndz. "It might be my mum."

We all put out our torches and lay down and pulled our sleeping bags over our heads and pretended to be fast asleep.

By now we were covered in goose bumps. We lay there waiting for the footsteps to go away, waiting for Lyndz's mum or dad to go back to bed, but they didn't. They just stood there for a moment.

Then, slowly, the door handle started to turn and the door started to open.

"Oh, help!" whispered Fliss. "I want my mum."

I wanted mine too. I slid down inside my sleeping bag and tried to block up my ears so I couldn't hear the next thing, but the room was so quiet you could have heard a feather drop.

Then there was the loudest hiccup I'd ever heard, or it could have been a burp. Something or somebody tripped over and fell headlong into the room and sprawled across the carpet. A funny deep voice said, "Who's that sleeping in my bed?"

It sounded just like one of the three bears. I thought, I've heard that voice before. I dared myself to look just as everyone else sat up and started squealing.

"Shhh, shhh!" hissed Lyndsey, turning on the light.

Lying there on the floor was her stupid brother. Not her stupid brother Tom, who'd already nearly given us forty fits with his face at the window. No, this was her other stupid brother, Stuart. He was lying on his back, grinning. His face was red and he looked sort of...

"Drunk! You're drunk," said Lyndz. "Stuart, get up this minute or I'll go and tell Dad. You're supposed to be sleeping in *my* bed."

"Oh, yes," he said, looking as if he could vaguely remember that arrangement. "Sorry," he mumbled. But he made no move. He just lay there on his back, like a whale. Then he closed his eyes and started snoring.

"Get up!" said Lyndsey. She crawled behind him and propped him up. He blinked, looked around and saw us all watching him, our eyes nearly out on stalks.

"Don't worry," he mumbled. "You all go back to sleep. I'll just go along to Lyndz's room." He rolled over onto all fours and sort of dragged himself up to a standing position. "Didn't mean to scare you." He swayed a bit and then, when he was steady enough, he backed out of the door and tiptoed along the landing. "Good night."

After he'd gone, we sat there for a minute staring at each other before anyone spoke. None of us had ever really seen anyone drunk before.

"I can't believe your brothers," I said.

"They're maniacs," said Kenny.

"They're idiots," said Rosie.

"Don't worry," said Lyndz. "They'll pay for it. Both of them." She started to think of all the things she could make them do for her: clean her riding boots, give her extra pocket money, take her turn at emptying the compost bucket. "If Dad finds out about this, he'll have fifty thousand fits. They'll be my slaves for weeks after this."

Now the excitement was over, Fliss said, "I think I'm going to be sick."

Fliss is always saying she's going to be sick. The trouble is, sometimes she is. We didn't know if this was one of those times. She certainly looked strange, but then we were all looking pretty strange by now.

"You'll be OK," said Lyndz. "If you just get to sleep, you'll be fine."

"I don't think I can get to sleep," she wailed.

"We'll help you," said Rosie. "We'll tell you a story."

"No more stories!" said Fliss. "It was probably those that made me feel sick in the first place."

"You need to take your mind off it. Think about something else."

"Like what?" said Fliss.

"Pistachio ice cream," said Lyndz.

Fliss sort of gulped and turned green. "P-lease."

Then I started to giggle, because I couldn't think of many things that looked more like a bowl of sick than pistachio ice cream. Kenny must have had the same idea because she started pretending to throw up. Then we all joined in. It was so stupid even Fliss burst out laughing.

"You're disgusting," she said. But she was starting to look better already.

"I'm hungry," said Lyndz. "We haven't had our midnight feast yet."

That was true, we hadn't. We'd all been so busy scaring ourselves silly, we'd forgotten about eating.

We heard the church clock down the road strike two o'clock as we sat there eating Black Jacks, Opal Fruits and Monster Munches. It was magic.

Then we snuggled down and turned out the lights and took it in turns to tell Fliss jokes, to keep her mind off feeling sick.

The last thing I remember was Kenny saying, "What do you give an elephant with big feet?"

And Rosie yawning and saying, "Lots of room."

GOODBYE

The next morning none of us could wake up. Even Lyndz slept in.

"Whatever time did you girls get to sleep?" Lyndz's mum asked us.

"Don't know," said Lyndz. "Didn't see the clock." Which was sort of true.

We were all feeling sick. No one could eat any breakfast. Lyndz's mum was really worried about Fliss. She still looked a funny colour. I felt *terrible*. But when my mum and dad came to collect me, I tried to pretend I was OK.

I gave them a big smile, but it felt as if my face was going to crack.

"Are you all right?" they asked, dead suspicious.

"Yeah," I said, lying through my teeth.

"Did you have a good time?"

"Yeah." But I couldn't keep it up. In fact, as soon as the car started, I was sick all over the back seat. So that was that. Mega trouble.

I told them it was probably the curry salad but they didn't believe me.

In fact, I haven't had a very nice week at all. I missed school on Monday and every day I keep on thinking about gremlins jumping out of cupboards and swinging from the lights and hiding under my bed. Scar-y.

But the good thing is, I suddenly remembered Winnie the Pooh. I was looking for something really cosy and safe to read in bed and I suddenly thought of Pooh and Piglet. I've reread all the stories and all the poems this week. It's nice, isn't it, finding old friends you'd forgotten? It's a good job I did, because I'm not allowed out.

Yep, grounded again. Just my luck. But so are all the others. Anyway, in the end, Lyndz let it out at home about Stuart coming home drunk, so he got in trouble with their dad, then she got in trouble with Stuart for telling on him.

But at least Lyndz found out it was Tom who'd been knocking on the wall, so that cleared up that mystery. Aren't brothers gruesome? We won't forget Lyndz's birthday sleepover in a hurry.

So, listen, take my advice, if you're going to watch a scary video, don't sit up telling horror stories *and* talking to ghosts *and* eating midnight feasts until two in the morning. Not if you want to keep in your parents' good books.

Uh-oh. There's my mum, looking for me now. I'd better go in before I get into any more trouble.

Remember: don't tell anyone what I've told you.

Now you've finished the book... eat it. See ya.

The Sleepover Club at Frankie's

Join the Sleepover Club: Frankie, Kenny, Felicity, Rosie and Lyndsey, five girls who just want to have fun – but who always end up in mischief.

Brown Owl's in a bad mood and the Sleepover Club are determined to cheer her up. Maybe she'd be happier if she had a new boyfriend. And where better than a sleepover at Frankie's to plan Operation Blind Date?

Pack up your sleepover kit and drop in on the fun!

0 00 675233 0

The Sleepover Club at Rosie's

Join the Sleepover Club: Frankie, Kenny, Felicity, Rosie and Lyndsey, five girls who just want to have fun – but who always end up in mischief.

The Pet Show should be really exciting for the girls except that Fliss doesn't have a pet! But, for the Sleepover Club who can outwit their dastardly enemies, the M&Ms, that shouldn't be a big problem – should it?

Pack up your sleepover kit and drop in on the fun!

0 00 675235 7

The Sleepover Club at Felicity's

Join the Sleepover Club: Frankie, Kenny, Felicity, Rosie and Lyndsey, five girls who just want to have fun – but who always end up in mischief.

A sleepover isn't a sleepover without a midnight feast and when the food runs out and everyone's still hungry, the Sleepover Club tiptoe down to the kitchen. But – quick! – the toaster's on fire!

Pack up your gleepover kit and drop in on the fun!

0 00 675236 5

Order Form

To order direct from the publishers, just make a list of the titles you want and fill in the form below:

Name

....

Address

....

....

....

Send to: Dept 6, HarperCollins Publishers Ltd, Westerhill Road, Bishopbriggs, Glasgow G64 2QT.

Please enclose a cheque or postal order to the value of the cover price, plus:

UK & BFPO: Add £1.00 for the first book, and 25p per copy for each additional book ordered.

Overseas and Eire: Add £2.95 service charge. Books will be sent by surface mail but quotes for airmail despatch will be given on request.

A 24-hour telephone ordering service is available to holders of Visa, MasterCard, Amex or Switch cards on 0141- 772 2281.

Collins
An *Imprint* of HarperCollins*Publishers*